Puppy in the Whitehouse

Raymond Paul Boyd

To order additional copies of this book, contact:
Xlibris
844-714-8691
www.Xlibris.com
Orders@Xlibris.com

ISBN: Softcover   978-1-6698-1682-9
       EBook   978-1-6698-1683-6

Print information available on the last page

Rev. date: 04/28/2022

"Puppy in the White House."

Child, and a puppy Jack Russell "Terrier." Named Wag had been given the singular privilege of reincarnation so he may perform his assignment he had been bestowed the title of Comforter to future president's of the United States of America. Manking him the only other creature that has the ability to reincarnate so their souls could achieve perfection.

Raymond Paul Boyd

It began with "the word" human beings have been
endowed by God with an every lasting soul attached with
free will. His benevolents was also bestow upon his lesser
creation of thoes that comprise the Animal Kingdom.
This story is a tidbit of how the two species co-exist.

In loving memory of my wife Gloria. 9-10-34 - 8-18-2000.

Dedicated to all who loves a story.

For-word

I Wag, "Comforter." Wish it to be known why for the first time I have refused to serve as Comforter to the present occupant the "forty fifth" in the White House. Due to his commitment to serve the dictates of the evil one. That I in good conscious, and exercising my gift of free will granted by the creator of all. But I'am encouraged that in the near future due to my ability of precognition I shall again serve in my capacity as conforte. In my true form a Jack Russell Terrier.

Foot Note.
My tail in the Animal Kingdom is 12" long. As it is with my breed

Puppy in the White House.

~~~~~~

Introduction

My name is "Wag." I have been summon to appear before "Bow-Wow" the supreme ruler of Animadom in the Great Hall. I hadn't a doubt as to why I was to be there. I was well aware that I had been remissed on several occasion in the performance of my assignments. That is to be a comfort to the Presidents of the United States of American. The first was George Washington, 1789-1796.

He and each proceeding president, had chosen the breed, and name of the puppy they desired. None were aware that my being with then had been predestine. Whether I'am allowed to continue in my capacity as a Comforter to future presidents, depends on the supreme Bow-Wow. The worse case possible is that I'am restricted from futher assignment, whitch I would regret deeply. Or hopefully I would be severely reprimanded. And alloyed to continue to serve as Comforter to the newly elected presidents and familes there is in our kingdom, of every creature, some of which are chosen to be Comforters of a select number of the human race. But unfortunately some of us allow ourselves to exhibit our disdain when we disagreed with their behavior, and I have been the worst offender. As I had watched many of the presidents practice the art of deceit. That which translates into the word "politics."

Foot Note. Magically I'am transform into whom ever of my kind the president selects. The moment he no longer is the president. I vacate, and repeat the process by inhabiting the next of my kind choosen by the next president.

Also, George Washington, had'nt been a resident of the White House, as it was built after his term in office.

Judgement

I stand in the Great Hall. The width and length of it extends. As far as the eye could see. The entrance is constructed of the great oak tree in the shape of an arch, the walls are trees of ivory, and pearched on their branchs are all manner of birds. A cloud of pink cotton candy sealed the top. The floor consisting of a layer of straw the color of pure gold. As the members of the Animal Kingdom entered, the straw floor does'nt yield to the weight of the visitors. We all looked in awe as Bow-Wow entered, unlike other shepherds, his coat is white, and glistens like snow. My coat is brown with spots of black.

Before Bow-Wow, began to speak I noticed that I was nervously wagging my tail. I quickly realized that doing so, Bow-Wow, would think I was expecting a compliment. Without shouting his voice was heard by everyone in the Great Hall. His tone of voice was without question compassionate. As he began to address why I was on trial. He then from memory began to

4

Recite all I had done. My first thought had been to plead guilty, and ask for another chance to be allow to continue my assignment as a Comforter. As I was about to speak my thoughts. Bow-Wow, looked at me, and said Wag. Although you are the one called to task this assembly is for the benefit of all the other Comforters whom like you allow their personal feeling to influence their behavior thus reacting negative to thoes they have been designated assignees, if I permit you to plead guilty, then the infractions that have been committed are overlooked. But then their are thoes that are more of a serious nature which can effect the Comforter and bring about dire consequence, and if the lapse of judgement isn't signaled out, then the lesson intended would be loss. Thus rendering this gather ineffective. Therefore we shall proceed, although it was I, and my conduct that was to be examined it was perfectly clear to me that I was being used as an example to other, that their future assignments were in jeopardy. I knew I had been derelict. Leniency was my only hope, and Bow-Wow, would see my sorrow.

Bow-Wow, glanced at me before he began to speak. A spontaneous shiver ran from my neck to my tail. I saw a twinkle from his eyes, of approval he was satisfied that his glance had the desired effect. I attempted to maintain eye contact. But I was overcomed with guilt, and shame. In stead I decided to concentrate on the limbs of the Ivory trees that extented the width, and length of the Great Hall, and in symmetrical order beginning with the small to the largest of every bird in existence. As were all others creatures, it was a phenomeaal sight to behold. I could not help but wonder if the other comfoters were feeling remorseful? I suspect they were Bow-Wow, had been precise in stating that I was not the only one remissed in proforming my duty with blemish. I did sense that they were relieved that it was I in stead of anyone of them. I tryed to mentally calculate the number of infraction I had committed during my time with each president? I could'nt. I was certain that Bow-Wow, knew, and would I also know.

I tensed when Bow-Wow, named the first George Washington, born in 1732, 1799. He was president, in the years, 1789-1796, Bow-Wow, raised his paw indicating he was about to speak. Instantly there was silence, and everyones ears perked up. That is to say thoes that have ears to perk up. Thoes that did'nt stared without blinking. Bow-Wow, begun by saying, their are in the human race whom are destine for greatness. Washington's, first job at 16, years of age. Was to take him on a surveying expedition in the Shenandoah Valley. Washington, had only a grade-school education, nor any military training. At six feet two inches, and well muscled, he was a strikingly imposing figure of a man. His passion was horse back riding, and fox hunting. By the time he was 21, years old the fact of war was inevitable. With the French.

Washington, was given the rank of Lieutenant Colonel. By the governor of Virginia. To protect the settlers with less then two hundred men. To stop the French to take over the Ohio settlement. With the help of Indian allies he was successful.

That was the start of the French and Indian war. Washington, distinguished himself in in the ensuing battles. With over a thousand men under his command. He was now twenty three years old. In 1758, he resigned from the army. To move to his home in Mount Vernon. A year later he married Martha Dandridge Custis, her wealth by far exceeded his own. Now with 6,500 acres, and one hundred plus slaves. Although the American Revolution War was on the far horizon. Washington, settled down to run his plantion thereby increasing his wealth. And enjoying his hobby of breeding his two dozen hounds for fox hunting. The British considerer the colnonies under their rule an imposed new taxes on imports. That resultsed in the Boston tea party. Washington, and other later to be known as the founding fathers of the declaration of Independence. It was agreed to accept Washington's proposal to boycott all goods from England. That decision made was inevitable. King George II ordered British troops to occupie Boston, in retaliation. Washington, was choosen commander of the army. It had taken Washington, less then a year to rout the British out of Boston. Washington's courageous stand at Pennsylvania's Valley Forge. Is what propelled him to become the first present of the Unite States. After his decline to stay in office he wanted to live out his life in Mount Vernon. Mr. Washington's plan to enjoy his leisure time to indulge his passion for fox hunting was not to be. Due to your misbehavior Wag, to act as Mr. Washington's comforter. Even though you were chosen above all of his hounds, to live inside of the home while twenty four others live in the kennels. Although you were the swift of all the others. You refused to join in the fox hunt. Also on two separate occasion you had bitten the hand of Mr. Washington, as a result of the infection that set in. Mr. Washington, was unable to hold the reins of his horse. Thereby he could no longer enjoy his pastime of fox hunting. Bow-Wow, then ask why I had violated my assignment as conforter? I was well aware before I replied he knew why I had acted so. It was for

the benefit of the others in attendance. I began by explaing that I did'nt wish to hunt for sport. The demise of foxs. Also I disapproved of the fact Mr. Washington, bought people, and used them as slaves. As I awaited Bow-Wow's, response, my tail again began to involuntarily Wag. The only thing I could do to stop it had been to sit on it. But to my amazement there was no chastisement forthcoming. Now I was confused, as I'am certain all the others in the Great Hall, I could hear their murmurs asking why Bow-Wow, was'nt saying anything? As I also awaited Bow-Wow's judgement, the weight of my body on my tail cause it to become numb. Although it's a contradiction in expression the feeling is quite uncomfortable, but my attention was diverted by Moo-Moo, the cow, asking what is the punisment for my misconduct? I and everyone was surprised by her audacity to question Bow-Wow. Are you so anxious not to wait to hear the full scope of this inquire before judgement is passed? Moo-Moo, did'nt respond. Not waiting for a reply. He continued. Next we have, John Adams, the 2nd, President, 1797-1801. Diplomacy was the Hallmark of John Adams, Presidency. He had been the first after it had been built to occupy the White House. Even though the construction had'nt been a hundred percent completed. Abigail, the wife of John Adams, had been involved in every aspect of her husband's presidency thus unabling her the capability to assist him with advice. That Adams found invaluable. Abigail, suffer a severe case of bronchitis, along with coughing spells, and fever. Dr. Rush, the attending physician employed the archaic practice of bleeding the patient. That resulted in the weaking of Abigail's, condition. Although Dr. Rush, had only performed the ritual twice it was then she decided to leave the White House, and return to their home in Massachusetts. Two months later Abigail, recovered completely, having relied on home remedies that consist of fruits, vegetables, and herbs. At Abigail's, suggestion Adams appointed their son John Quincy, to be the Ambassador of Prussia.

President Adams, wanted a navy that would be sufficient to protect the country. And he was also against slavery. Having completed his synopsis Bow-Wow, looked at me, and asked why had I bitten Dr. Rush.? I had hoped he would not had ask me that question as I had been without fault in my devotion to President John Adam's. I could see all eyes were focused on me. I was well aware as usual that Bow-Wow, had known the answer to the question, therefore I addressed my reply to thoes in attendances, and said with pride because his treatment put the life of Mrs. Adams at risk.

That's a very good reason. Bow-Wow, said. Having hear what appeared to be Bow-Wow's approval of my reason I was applauded with roars, and howls. Just when I was about to raise my paws in triumph, the Great Hall, became abruptly silent as the "but" muted the sounds of my compadres. Spoken by Bow-Wow, he then gently chastised me saying that my act of violence could'nt be justified.

As I awaited what I considered a lengthy reprimand, I was delighted to hear. Bow-Wow, say lets proceed with Wag's 8. Years with the third presiend, Thomas Jefferson. Wag, you were a terrier. One of his major accomplishments he had drafted the declaration of Idependence. It had been believed by many it would be the catalyst to the abolishment of slavery. But alas it was not to be, I thought it was ironic that the signatorys themselves owned slaves. Jefferson's prize possession was his home he named Monticello that he had designed. One of the statutes of the State of Virginia Jefferson had author. Religious Freedom. Bow-Wow, then addressed the fact I had been willful in my behavior towards President Jefferson. In spite of his accomplishments, and should'nt had'nt overlooked President Jefferson freeing many of his slaves. I replied in defense saying had I understood the wisdom of what he had said, I had wanted at that very moment to have bitten my tongue, but that was an impossibility in this realm of existence as not I nor anyone could inflict pain on self or others, but one did have the ability to express sorrow. I did realize as I stood before Bow-Wow. That I was flawed in humility. "Foot-note" "John Adams. Died July 4th 1826. Five hours after Jefferson." Now let us proceed to your next assignment. That of James Madison, 4th President of Unite States. 1809-1817. He had been the principal framer of the constitution. The eight years of your time had been without incident. Bow-Wow, acknowledgement gave me a feeling of satisfaction. I was a French Poodle in that re-incarnation chosen by his wife Dolly.

Bow-Wow, then began to recite a brief summary of James Monroe, election the 5th President, 1817-1825. One of his many accomplishments had been to persuade the congress for the nationalization of an army for the protection of the Unite States. Bow-Wow concluded by stating once again that I had performed my assignment without incident. His statement was greeted with an ovation of applause. I was overcome with pride, I control my impulse to smile, but I again I had been unable to prevent my tail from wagging vigorously. I was a Spaniel at that point in time. Bow-Wow's ears stiffen that was an indication he was about to speak, and there was silence in the Great Hall. He looked at me, and said Wag. Need I remind you that a review of your tenure in the White House has just begun, and I suggest everyone delay their show of approval until Wag's final assignment has been assessed.

Bow-Wow's words caused my tail to cease, and stiffen. Before Bow-Wow, began I had wished he would had just summarized my entire assignment and spear me the embarrassment of reliving the fact I had'nt perform my duty as expected, even though I understood that time as in the spirit world of mankind is irrelevant. Never the less my guilt weighed heavy on my conscious. I knew Bow-Wow, was aware of my state of mind. He then looked at me, and smiled I understood it was ment to bolster my confidence. Now we come to the 6th President, John Quincy Adams. Elected 1825-1829. Son of the 2nd President of the United States. One of his most notable speech was addressing the abolishment of slavery. Stating that it would not be exterminated because of thoes who knew it to be morally wrong. And that the issue would be settled by armed conflict between the south, and north. History had proven him correct. But the war did'nt solve the problem of bigotry. But it was a step towards the equality of mankind. Bow-Wow, having completed his brief narrative, said to the spectators, need I address what our brother Wag's reaction on President, John Quincy Adams final day in offic at the White House?

They replied in unison. Our brother Wag, bit the president. I dont know why in response I took a bow. Of course a moment later I realized the absurdity of what I had did, and was about to apolgize, but I was prevented from doing so, by the raising of Bow-Wow's paw.

Abraham Lincoln, the 16th, President. Your affection towards him was commendable.

The day following Mr. Lincoln's assassination you bitten his wife. I was tempted to justify why I had done so. But I remained silent. As I saw that Bow-Wow, and all the other were expecting my reply, I paused, pardon the "pun." To re think my decision not explain why I had bitten the hand of Mrs. Lincoln.

I was also persuaded by the assembly that awaited my response. Without further ado, I related why I had once again neglected not to interfere with human beings. I begun by explaining that we of the Animal Kingdom are gifted with the sensibility within minutes of a catastrophic event such as an earthquake, and storms that create havoc upon the earth. But as I listen to the mild objection of the president, speaking to his wife, explaining that it was urgent he present a budget to the congress that would compensate the veterans of the civil was in some small measure for their sacrifice, as well for the families of the deceased. That would include both sides of the conflict. And that he would gladly attend the final performance at Ford Theater, "Of Our American Cousin." But I knew he would succumb to his wife's demand. I slinked unobserved from the oval office, and went to the master bedroom there the only thing I could think of had been to hide the president's stove pipe hat, I had intended to take it into another room. But that had been precluded by the oncoming of foot steps by the Lincolns with haste I dragged it under the bed. As they entered I felt I had averted what I belived to be something that would harm the president. I sat pleased by the side of the massive bed, as the president inquired of his wife the whereabouts of his hat? In response to the question I was swiftly slaped twice on my rump. Causing me to think she had psychic powers. She knelt by the side of the bed as I yelp vacating in pain exposing a portion of the hat. I believe the fate of the president may had been altered if only I had taken his hat out of the bedroom. As always I had the need to justify myself.

Bow-Wow, unexpectedly offerer not a word of comment concerning what I had said in my defense. He gazed at me for a moment then at all in the Great Hall, said to avoid repetition I shall address Wag's time with Franklin D. Roosevelt. The 32nd U.S. President. 1933-1945. During that time our brother Wag, incarnated as a Scottish Terrier named "Fala." It was a time of the great depression and unfortunately "World War Two." I'am delighted to proclaim that Wag's, assignment had been outstanding in the service as a companion to the president in the most of difficult times of world history. No other president had been in enguled in the turbulent up-heaval. Therefore the question of equality had'nt been addressed. It was on the agenda postwar the president had planed to sign it into the Law of the Land Confident with the support of the congress. His sudden demise in 1945 precluded that, Harry S. Truman the Vice President, as mandated by law became the 33rd President of the U.S.A. 1945-1953. Pres. Truman, had intended to implement a Bill of Equal Rights in accordance with the wish of President, Roosevelt. But the burden of having sanction the use of the atom bomb in Japan to end the 2nd World War greatly depressed him, but Wag. Now a Cocker Spaniel named Feller performed his obligation as Comforter, but the demans put upon Pres. Truman were such he had been unable to implement a Bill of Rights during his term in the office of president. Now just as Bow Wow, had been about to speak on the subject of Wag's objection of incarnating of other then himself known in the world as "Jack Russell." But was interrupted by Chi-Chi, the monkey that had been hanging his two foot body by his three and a half long foot tail from the branch of the Ivory tree. With the use of one one his equal long arms he snatched a banana from the vine. That magically was replaced by another as well a cluster of peanuts Chi-Chi, had also grabbed. A moment after devouring the succulent fruit, he ask if he could have the position of Comforter in the earths plain? No. Bow-Wow, replied. Chi-Chi, knew the Great Shepherd's reply was'nt debatable. Stuffing the cluster of peanuts into his mouth he swung away. Ronald the duck waddle up to

Bow-Wow, with the same request. Yes you may, that is if you have not an aversion to being roasted, and served for Sunday dinner, that most certainly would comfort the president's appetite. He said with a twinkle and smile. Thank you no. Sir replied Ronald, as he with haste waddled away for fear Bow-Wow, would have change of mind. All stood in amazement as Bow-Wow, grew 2' taller as he said, without further more interruption I would ask that all of you that enjoy the never ending abundance of fruits, and vegetables, pay homage to our creator. And miraculously there is'nt need to excrete what's eaten or drank. Now before I continue to address the business at hand, I see our brother Chi-Chi, is speaking to Albert, "The Owl."

I assume Chi-Chi, has need to an answer to a question. I shall allow a moment. Bow-Wow said with a knowing smile. Albert, perceived Chi-Chi,'s question before it had been asked, said the reason Bow-Wow had'nt explained why he said no, the fact is you had been in the earth three times and each time you were eaten by Chimpanzee as a source of protein. Bow-Wow had wished to spare you the memory. Now do you still desire to have your request granted? No, Chi-Chi, replied. In the heavenly Animal Kingdom every word spoken is heard. Albert, then suggest we give a rousing applause for Bow-Wow, whom has wisdom that serves us all. There was a thundering ovation, Bow-Wow, with the raising of his right paw he signaled for silence and said with all humility I thank you all. Next we have the 34th U.S. President, Dwight D. Eisenhower. Wag, in that reincarnation. You were a Weimaraner, named Heidi. During that time you served well. Next the 35th President, 1961-63 John F. Kennedy, Wag, at that time you were one of ten Comforters, you as a German Shepherd, named Clipper.

You are to be commended as you saw to the behavior of the others. Again you have served with honor. But the president whom had promised Rev. Martin Luther King, that he would put forth a Bill of Racial Equality. But fate had intervened, President Kennedy had suffered the same fate as Abraham Lincoln. Now we come to the 36th U.S Presiden, Lydon B. Johnson, "1963-69," it was when you took possession of Edgar his beagle.

That Pres. Johnson, signed the equal rights amendment, even so there were many that maintained their bias. And once again our brother Wag is guilty of having bitten the the president. Bow-Wow, paused as he surveyed the Great Hall. I was well aware that Bow-Wow, had waited for me to explain. I debated for a moment, and with confidence I felt justified for having disregarded my assignment as Comforter. I simply stated that I as Edgar, had often been liften by my ears, and hearing him say when question by reporters, reply with laughter that it was good for me. Thinking that I vindicated mysele I gazed into the eyes of Bow-Wow. Certain he would approve of what I had done he stared back at me, I was unable to maintain eye contact all in the Great Hall looked in awe with an expectation of a reply from Bow-Wow.

I and so were thy taken aback. When Bow-Wow, continued saying, Richard M. Nixon, the 37th person to occupy the office of president. Stated that our brother "Wag" was a Poodle, named Pasha, a Terrier. During his term, 1969-74. Wag, you had bitten him 4, times, there isn't a doubt it would have been more if he were not impeached. Next Gerald R. Ford took the office as the 38th. U.S. President. 1974-1977. Wag, you inhabited a Golden Retriever, named Liberty. During that time you remained aloof. Therefore your time had been unevenful. So it's deemed you were re-miss. But had snapped at him twice. I was taken aback by Bow-Wow asking if I had wish to comment? I must say I was tongue-tied. As I tried to decide to reply,? Several moments elapse as I gazed at those in the Great Hall. As I did so I could feel the eyes of Bow-Wow on me.

What-to do? As I pounder. The question, when the distinct gruff voice of squeeze the python, raising himself up to his full height of thirty feet asked why I'am not answering Bow-Wow question? Yes why not? Hug, the bear stop for a moment mumching on a vine of blue berries, said yes I second the question. I knew if I answered I would be admitting again I was derelict of my duty as a Comforter, by given sway to my emotion of my dislike of President Ford, having granting a pardon to President Nixon, for his misdeeds. Not waiting if I were to reply, hug bear

begun to gord himself eating the succlent fruit of the vine continuously replaced. I then looked up at Bow-Wow, and said Please excuse me I wish not to say at this time. Then let us continue, Bow-Wow, replied, assuring every one the questions and the impending ones would be revisit at the conclusion of my examination of our brother Wag. That's good enough for me, shouted Stripes the tiger. Hah-hah, the hyena laughing said he was also in agreement. Bow-Wow, stared knowingly at me for a second. That look "To coin a phrase told me I was'nt off the hook." Bow-Wow, begun, saying our brother's time with Jimmy D. Carter, 39th President. "1977-1981" as an Afghan Hound, Wag, I must say were quite rude to him as you failed to obey him. I without thinking I defended my self by saying that's because I did'nt think he was effective as a president. At that moment I knew I should had put my paw in my mouth. Bow-Wow, gave me a look of disapproval.

Without a word of rebuke Bow-Wow, continued. "I must admit his look caused my heart to skip several beats." I listen as he said I'am not going to elaborate on Ronald R. Reagan, 40th President. 1981-89 as he had Wag, and six other Comforters. 3, of which were our sisters. Having said that he slowly surveyed the audience, and then addressed me asking if I had any negative remarks as your time had been spent frolicking with the other Comforters? I replied with pride, saying President Reagan, was a great speaker, but his promise to help the people, only fueled the rich. Again Bow-Wow ignored my remarks.

This time he only glanced at me, as he continued re-calling my time with the remaining presidents. George H. W. Bush, 41st to be elected 1989-1993. As a femal Spaniel, Wag, had bitten both the president and his wife. Bow-Wow, made no further comment, nor did I. Next Bill D. Clinton, became the 42nd President. 1993-2001. Wag as Labrador, I'am proud to say his behavior had been without fault. Needless to say my tail wagged beyond my control. The appaluse, and the sound of stomping feet fed my ego. Bow-Wow, waited a full minute. Then to my surprise also I'm certain to everyone else he barked once if created the sound of clapping thunder the effect was instant silence something I had never witnessed before. Now that I have everyones attention I shall remind all of you that this examination has yet concluded. Bow-Wow, then said in a tone of voice that was benevolent assured all they would shortly have the opportunity to approve or disapprove what has been revealed. George W. Bush the 43rd, President. 2001-2009. Wag, was a Scottish Terrier at that time, during your stay you remained aloof, that I'm sure you have a justification to explain why? Barack Obama, 44th

President. 2009-2017. As a Portugueses water dog, named Bo, Wag's conduct has earn an "A." Bow-Wow. With his right paw raised everyone including myself understood there was to be no response. Bow-Wow, smiled, and said Now I shall elaborate the importance of being a Comforter to the men that had been elected to the highest office in the Unite States of America. Now I shall explain why our brother Wag, had been derelict at times in his assignment. The fact of the matter is our brother Wag, allowed himself to be caught up in the politics of the human race, in particular the stance of a number of president's on equal rights. Due to the efforts of President Abraham Lincoln, and President Lyndon B. Johnson. It's now the Law of the Land. Even so man has yet to find it in their heart to exist in harmony. Therfore I have decided that our brother Wag's assignment as Comforter is hearby recinded. He shall remain with us as himself a Jack Russell. Now that for the time being concludes the business at hand unless someone has something to say? I do if I may said Corkie the pig hunched waving his two front legs? And what is that? Ask Bow-Wow, Corkie, replied with a smile of pride, saying I'am well suited to take brother Wag's place as Comforter. And why is that? Bow-Wow, asked with an expression of curiosity. Corkie, replied saying as he looked surveying the Great Hall and then his eyes fixed on Bow-Wow, in all modesty it's a fact that I have an exceptional I.Q. therefore I would like very much be the next Comforter to the President of the United States.

Bow-Wow, looked down

at Corkie, shaking his head slowly and said in a tone of voice obviously sympathetic my dear brother it's also a fact the president is partial to bar-b-q. spear ribs. The thought of what Bow-Wow, had said caused Corkie to shiver as he slowly walked away mumbling a thank you. Bow-Wow, then said as an after though addressing me for all to hear, although equal rights is now law it's capitalized in the embodiment of the election of Barack Obama, but the eradication of prejudice, that's embedded in the hearts of many of the human race. That I can assure you shall be reconciled by the creator of all.

There was a thunder of cheers.

Suddenly all were instantly quiet as their attention was attracted by the sound of the twenty bull elephants clearing their throats in preparation with a thousand birds of assorted species to begin to sing, Handel's Messiah. To be conducted by Saint Francis, formerly of Assisi. He raised his arms holding a baton in his right hand he tapped the lectern twice. With smile he began to conduct. The singing was magnificent, the crescendo trumpeted by the elephants, a symphony without equal. Immensely enjoyed by all in God's heaven ajacent to the Animal Kingdom.

Ever and ever,
"Amen."

Books published by the author:

The Alpha, 'Dracula'

The President's Wife

It's Who You Know

The Log Cabin

The Shadow of Paradise

E-mail to Heaven

The Judgement of Sarah Solomon

Condemnation

Laraine Day F.B.I

Eternal Love

Wag and the Judgement of Bow-Wow

It's inherent to crave domination by a vast number of people. Over others if not so the population would enjoy a life of peace and harmony.

Footnote
Raymond Paul Boyd